Once there was a soft brown toy called Dogger.
One of his ears pointed upwards and the other
flopped over. His fur was worn in places because
he was quite old. He belonged to Dave.

Dave was *very* fond of Dogger. He took him everywhere.

Sometimes he gave him rides in a trolley.

Sometimes he pulled him along on a lead made of string like a real dog.

When it was cold he wrapped him up in a bit of blanket.

DOGGER

The much-loved story about finding your favourite toy

Shirley Hughes

Red Fox

For Judy and Margaret

Also by Shirley Hughes

RED FOX

UK | USA | Canada | Ireland | Australia | India | New Zealand | South Africa

Red Fox is part of the Penguin Random House group of companies
whose addresses can be found at global.penguinrandomhouse.com.
www.penguin.co.uk   www.puffin.co.uk   www.ladybird.co.uk

Penguin
Random House
UK

First published 1977
This edition published 2017
001

Copyright © Shirley Hughes, 1977
With story read by Olivia Colman
Copyright in this recording ℗ Penguin Books Ltd, 2017

A CIP catalogue record for this book is available from the British Library

Printed in China

ISBN: 978–1–782–95727–0

FSC
www.fsc.org

MIX
Paper from
responsible sources
FSC® C018179

Now and again Dave's
Mum said that Dogger was
getting much too dirty. She showed Dave how to
wash him in a bowl of soapy water. Then they
hung him up by his tail on the washing-line to dry.

Dave's baby brother, Joe, liked hard toys. He liked putting them in his mouth and biting on them, because he was getting teeth.

Dave's big sister, Bella, took seven teddies to bed
with her every night. She had to sleep right up
against the wall to stop herself from falling out.
But Dave liked only Dogger.

One afternoon Dave and Mum set out to collect
Bella from school. Mum took Joe in the pushchair
and Dave took Dogger. Next to the school gate
where the mums waited was a playing-field. Some
men with ladders were putting up coloured flags.
Mum said that there was going to be a Summer
Fair to get money to buy things for the school.
Dave pushed Dogger up against the railings to
show him what was going on.

Just then the children started to come out of
school. An ice-cream van came round the corner
playing a tune. Bella ran up with her satchel flying.
   "Mum, can we have an ice-cream?"
   Mum gave her the money for two cones. Joe
didn't have a whole ice-cream to himself because
he was too dribbly.

On the way home Dave walked beside
the pushchair giving Joe licks off his
ice-cream. Joe kicked his feet about and
shouted for more in-between licks.

At tea-time Dave was rather quiet.
In the bath he was even quieter.
At bed-time he said:
"I want Dogger."
But Dogger was nowhere to be found.

Mum looked under the bed.

She looked behind the cupboard.

She searched in the kitchen—

—and underneath the stairs.
Dave watched anxiously through
the banisters. Joe watched
through the bars of his cot.

Bella joined in to look for Dogger. She turned out
her own toy-box in case he was in there, but he
wasn't.

When Dad came home he looked for Dogger
too. He searched in the shed and down the garden
path with a torch.

But Dogger was quite lost.

Dave was very sad when he went to bed. Bella
kindly lent him one of her teddies to go to sleep
with but it was not the same thing as Dogger.
Dave kept waking up in the night and missing
him.

The next day was Saturday and they all went to the School Summer Fair. The playing-field was full of stalls and side-shows.

There was a Fancy Dress Parade.

Then there were Sports, with an Egg-and-Spoon Race—

a Wheelbarrow Race

and a Fathers' Race.

Bella was very good at races.
She won the Three-Legged Race
with her friend Barbara.
   "Wouldn't you like to go in
for a race?" they asked Dave.
But Dave didn't feel like racing.
He was missing Dogger
too much.

Then another very exciting thing happened to
Bella. She won first prize in a Raffle! It was a huge
yellow Teddy Bear, wearing a beautiful blue silk
bow. He was almost as big as Dave.

Dave didn't like that Teddy at all. At that
moment he didn't like Bella much either because
she kept on winning things. He went off on his
own to look at the stalls.

One lady had a Toy Stall, full of knitted ducks
and cars and baby dolls in bonnets. And there,
at the very back of the stall, behind a lot of
other toys, was ——

DOGGER!

He was wearing a ticket saying "5p".

There were a lot of people round the stall. Dave tried to explain to the lady that it was his Dogger, who had got lost and somehow been put on the stall by mistake, but she wasn't listening. He looked in his pocket. He had 3p but that wasn't enough. He ran to find Mum and Dad to ask them to buy Dogger back *at once*.

Dave went everywhere in the crowd but he couldn't see Mum and Dad. He thought he was going to cry. At last he found Bella by the cakes. When she heard about Dogger, she and Dave ran back to the Toy Stall as fast as they could.

But something terrible
had happened. Dogger had
just been bought by
a little girl!

She was already walking
off with him. Dave began to cry.

Bella ran after her and
tried to explain that
Dogger really belonged
to Dave, and could they
please buy him back?

But the little girl said:
"No."

She said that she had
bought Dogger with her
own money and she
wanted him. She held
on to him very tightly.

Dave cried and cried.

    And the little girl started to cry too.

    But out of the corner of her eye she caught sight of Bella's big yellow Teddy. She stopped crying and put out her hand to stroke his beautiful blue silk bow.

Then Bella did something *very* kind.

"Would you swop this Teddy for my brother's dog, then?" she asked. Right away the little girl stopped crying and began to smile. She held out Dogger to Dave, took the big Teddy instead and went off with him in her arms.

Then Dave smiled too.

He hugged Dogger and he hugged Bella round the waist.

"Thank you, Bella," he said.

That night Dave had Dogger in bed beside him.
   Bella was practising somersaults.
   "Shall you miss that big Teddy?" Dave asked her.
   "No," said Bella, "I didn't like him much really.
He was too big and his eyes were too staring.
Anyway if I had another Teddy in my bed there
wouldn't be room for me."